EDDYCAT
Helps Sunshine Plan Her Party

For a free color catalog describing Gareth Stevens's list of high-quality books, call 1-800-341-3569 (USA) or 1-800-461-9120 (Canada).

Library of Congress Cataloging-in-Publication Data

Barnett, Ada.
    Eddycat helps Sunshine plan her party / by Ada Barnett, Pam Manquen, and Linda Rapaport ; illustrated by Mark Hoffmann.
       p. cm. -- (Social skill builders for children)
    Summary: Her mother helps Sunshine plan her birthday party, while across town Buddy's father instructs him on how to behave as a party guest. At intervals in the text, Eddycat makes additional comments about party etiquette.
    ISBN 0-8368-0942-4
    [1. Parties--Fiction. 2. Etiquette--Fiction. 3. Animals--Fiction.] I. Manquen, Pam. II. Rapaport, Linda. III. Hoffmann, Mark, ill. IV. Title. V. Series.
PZ7.B2629Ed   1993
[E]--dc20   92-56880

Published by
Gareth Stevens Publishing
1555 North RiverCenter Drive, Suite 201
Milwaukee, Wisconsin 53212, USA

This edition of *Eddycat Helps Sunshine Plan Her Party* was first published in the USA and Canada by Gareth Stevens, Inc., in association with The Children's Etiquette Institute. Text, artwork, characters, design, and format © 1993 by The Children's Etiquette Institute.

Sincere thanks to educators Jody Henderson-Sykes of Grand Avenue Middle School in Milwaukee, Wisconsin, and Mel Ciena of the University of San Francisco for their invaluable help.

Printed in the United States of America

1 2 3 4 5 6 7 8 9 98 97 96 95 94 93

Children's Etiquette Institute

Social Skill Builders for Children

EDDYCAT

EDDYCAT
Helps Sunshine Plan Her Party

Gareth Stevens Publishing
MILWAUKEE

CONTENTS

Hi, friends! Remember me? I'm Eddycat, and I live in the city of Mannersville.

Everyone here believes there is something special about certain words and sentences because they make others smile and feel good.

My goal is to try to make the world a better place in which to live, but I need your help. What you need to do is let others know that you care about them and that you care about yourself. I will show you the special way of doing this. And it will make me very happy to cheer you on as you learn to say the special words and follow the special rules!

Today, I am going to help Sunshine plan her birthday party. In addition, Buddy Brownbear will learn how to be a wonderful guest. If you pay close attention, you will learn, too.

Here are some of the special phrases and magical words used in this Eddycat story. Can **you** find these words and sentences in the story?

Good morning.   *I'm proud.*
Good-bye.   *Thank you.*
Please.   *I hope you will join us.*

It is a beautiful, bright spring day in Mannersville when Mother Smithbear awakens her daughter, Sunshine.

"Good morning, Sunshine. It's time to get up. Today is the day we are going to plan your birthday party!" says Mother Smithbear.

"The first thing we should do, Sunshine, is decide how many guests you want to invite. Then we'll make a list of their names," says Mother Smithbear.

It helps to make a list of things to do in order to prepare for the party. Sunshine must decide on which games to play at the party and which prizes she is going to give out.

On the invitations Sunshine is going to send, she has included an R.S.V.P. section. The letters *R.S.V.P.* mean "Please reply." Sunshine must decide whether she wants a "telephone" R.S.V.P. or a "written" R.S.V.P.

When you see a telephone number next to an R.S.V.P., it means that calling the host/hostess on the telephone is the best way to reply. If there is no telephone number, then your reply should be sent through the mail in the form of a note.

If you are going to be seating guests at a table, it is always a good idea to make a place card with each guest's name on it.

At a party, always have plenty to eat and drink for your guests. Also, have something special on hand for your friends who may have allergies to certain foods and drinks.

It is thoughtful to have substitute foods and drinks available so that your friends with allergies do not feel left out.

ICE CREAM

NON-DAIRY FROZEN DESSERT

It is fun to dress up for a party to make the occasion special!

Across town in Mannersville, Mr. Mailman delivers Sunshine's invitation to Buddy Brownbear's house.

I'm proud of Sunshine because she invited the new boy in town to her party. It is always nice to help new friends meet others so they will feel welcome.

This is a happy day for Buddy Brownbear. He has received his first party invitation ever!

Pay attention, Buddy. You are about to learn how to be a wonderful guest!

Mother Brownbear explains to Buddy that the R.S.V.P. on the invitation means that he needs to let Sunshine know if he will be coming to the party. Then Sunshine will be able to shop for the right amount of ice cream and cake for the party.

Buddy's father takes Buddy to the store to buy a birthday gift for Sunshine. Buddy likes to look at cars and trucks.

Father Brownbear explains to Buddy that when shopping for a gift, it is important to try to find something the other person will really like.

"Buddy, you know Sunshine likes to read in her free time. What type of book do you think she might be interested in?" asks Father Brownbear.

"I can see that choosing the right gift takes a lot of thought," says Buddy.

Buddy knows that Sunshine also likes flowers.
He chooses a book that he knows she will like.
It is a picture book of flowers—the perfect gift!

It always feels special to take a beautifully wrapped package to a friend.

Finally, it is the day of the party! Buddy knows it is important for him to do the following:

1. Shower or take a bath, and...

2. comb his hair, and...

3. clean his fingernails, and...

4. brush his teeth, and...

5. polish his shoes, and...

6. dress neatly.

Buddy likes to look his best when he is going somewhere special. Buddy needs help with this now. But when he grows up, he will shine his shoes and dress well, all on his own.

Getting ready for a party is a lot of fun if everyone pitches in and helps out.

Sunshine's brother, Seymour, rakes and...

picks up his toys.

Eddycat vacuums and...

takes out the garbage.

Sunshine bakes cookies, and...

Father Smithbear decorates.

Can you think of something you can do to help get ready for a party?

Sunshine says happily, "Thank you everyone for helping me get ready for my birthday party. I can hardly wait for the guests to arrive on Saturday!"

Sunshine and I want to thank you for helping us get ready for the party. Isn't it fun learning how to plan things correctly so that everyone will have a good time and feel welcome? Good-bye for now. I hope you will join us at Sunshine's party!

EDDYCAT'S HELPFUL TERMS

apologize
To say you are sorry when you have made a mistake.

cleanliness
Being sure you are clean and neatly dressed.

etiquette
The special rules for how to behave and treat others.

guest list
A list of people who are invited to a party.

invitation
A card that invites someone to a party or other event.

place cards
Small cards, each with a guest's name written on it, located at each place setting at a table.

"Please."
A word used to politely request something.

R. S. V. P.
An abbreviation of a French phrase that means "Répondez s'il vous plaît" or "Please respond."

table manners
Special rules for eating politely.

taking turns
Making sure everyone gets an equal chance to play a game or take part in an activity.

MORE BOOKS TO READ

The *Eddycat* series is the only truly authoritative collection on etiquette written for children. Nonetheless, the additional titles by other authors listed here represent good support for the concept that courtesy and manners are valuable skills and habits.

Nonfiction:
Eddycat and Buddy Entertain a Guest. Barnett, Manquen, Rapaport (Gareth Stevens)
Eddycat Attends Sunshine's Birthday Party. Barnett, Manquen, Rapaport (Gareth Stevens)
Eddycat Goes Shopping with Becky Bunny. Barnett, Manquen, Rapaport (Gareth Stevens)
Eddycat Introduces. . . Mannersville. Barnett, Manquen, Rapaport (Gareth Stevens)
Eddycat Teaches Telephone Skills. Barnett, Manquen, Rapaport (Gareth Stevens)

Good Manners for Girls and Boys. Hickman (Crown)
My First Party Book. Wilkes (Knopf)
What Do You Say? A Child's Guide to Manners. Snell (David and Charles)
Your Manners Are Showing. Baker (Child's World)

Fiction:
Dinner at Alberta's. Hoban (Harper)
Going to a Party. Civardi and Cartwright (EDC)

PLACE TO WRITE

For more information about etiquette, write to the American Etiquette Institute, P.O. Box 700508, San Jose, CA 95170.

PARENT/TEACHER GUIDE

allergies   page 11

It is thoughtful of the host/hostess to provide special foods and drinks for guests who have allergies. However, he or she is not obligated to do so. Therefore, if you do have food allergies, it is helpful to bring your own food along. Let the host/hostess know what you will be bringing so as to avoid any last-minute confusion.

clothes   pages 12, 23

Guests dress up for a party or other event to help make the occasion special. Clothes should be appropriate for the time, place, and occasion. Most importantly, a guest should be neat and clean.

gift-giving   pages 17-20

When a gift is given, it is important to buy something the person will like – not something you might want for yourself. Establish a price prior to arriving at the store. The important thing is not the amount of money spent, but rather the thought-fulness of the gift. It is better to buy one small, well-made item than several larger items of poor quality. A carefully wrapped package conveys the message, "I care." Pets should never be given as a gift without prior approval from the parents of the recipient.

personal hygiene   pages 12, 21, 22

Teaching children about personal hygiene at a very young age can save them painful embarrassment and rejection throughout their lives. A toothbrush and toothpaste, nail file, nail brush, comb, brush, and soap are easy to learn to use at a young age.

place cards page 10

Place cards may be used at any meal. They indicate to guests where the host/hostess wants them to sit, and they inform guests how to address the others in attendance. A basic place card of plain white cardboard is always correct. It should be approximately 2 inches (5 centimeters) by 1.5 inches (3.8 centimeters). It may be a foldover card or a single piece of cardboard. A place card stands in back of the plate and is never moved by anyone other than the host or hostess.

R.S.V.P. pages 9, 14, 16

R.S.V.P. is French for "Répondez s'il vous plaît." In English, it means "Please reply." (If the words "Please reply" are used on an invitation, do not abbreviate those words.) Either R.S.V.P. or R.s.v.p. is correct. When these letters, or words, appear on an invitation, an answer must be given – either acceptance or rejection. Reply as soon as possible so that party plans can be made. If there is an address only, the answer should be sent in the mail. If a telephone number is given, a telephone call should be made.

INDEX